Houghton Mifflin Science
DISCOVERYWORKS

WORKBOOK

INVESTIGATION REVIEWS

HOUGHTON MIFFLIN

Boston • Atlanta • Dallas • Denver • Geneva, Illinois • Palo Alto • Princeton

CONTENTS

LIFE CYCLES

Name _________________________________ Date _________________

1. Study the pictures of a dog. These pictures represent different stages in the life cycle of a dog. Number the stages in the correct order by labeling them 1, 2, 3, and 4.

_______   _______   _______   _______

2. Use the words in the box and the clues to complete the puzzle.

adult	baby	child	cycle	teenager

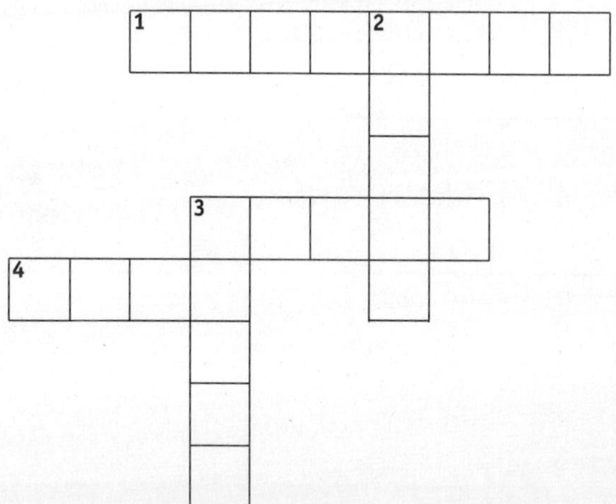

Across

1. The stage a person is in when he or she is 14 years old

3. The stage you are in now

4. The first stage of a person

Down

2. The stage a grown-up is in

3. All of the stages of growth are part of a life _____.

Process Skills
Inferring

Look at the drawing of a mother dog and her puppy. List three traits that were passed on from the mother dog to the puppy. List one learned trait for the puppy. How are traits that are passed on different from learned traits? Write your answer on another sheet of paper.

Answers on
Assessment Guide p. 147

Name _________________________   Date _________________________

1. Use the words in the box to label the
drawing below of the chicken egg.

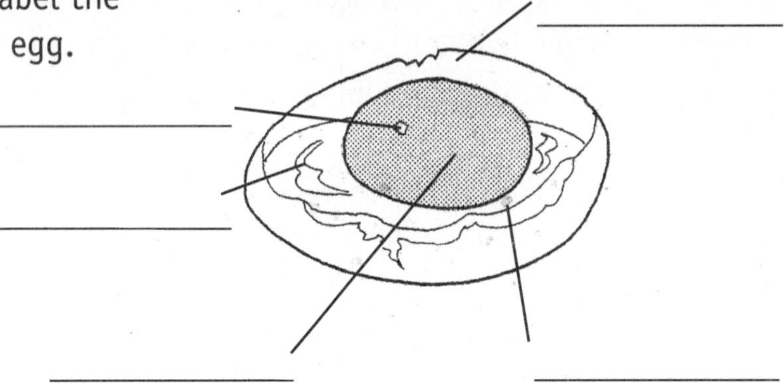

egg white
shell
shell lining
white spot
yolk

2. Use the words in the box to complete the chart that
tells the purpose of each part of a chicken egg.

| egg white | shell | white spot | yolk |

Develops into a Bird	Protects the Developing Bird	Serves as a Food Source for the Developing Bird

Process Skills
Classifying

On another sheet of paper, make a chart
with two columns. Title one column
"Animals That Lay Eggs." Title the other
column "Animals That Do Not Lay Eggs."
Fill in your chart by classifying which of
the following animals lay eggs and which
do not.

crocodile	bald eagle
chicken	elephant
wallaby	owl
horse	starfish
penguin	

Answers on
Assessment Guide p. 147

Name _________________________________ Date _______________

1. Label the stages in the life cycle of a mealworm.

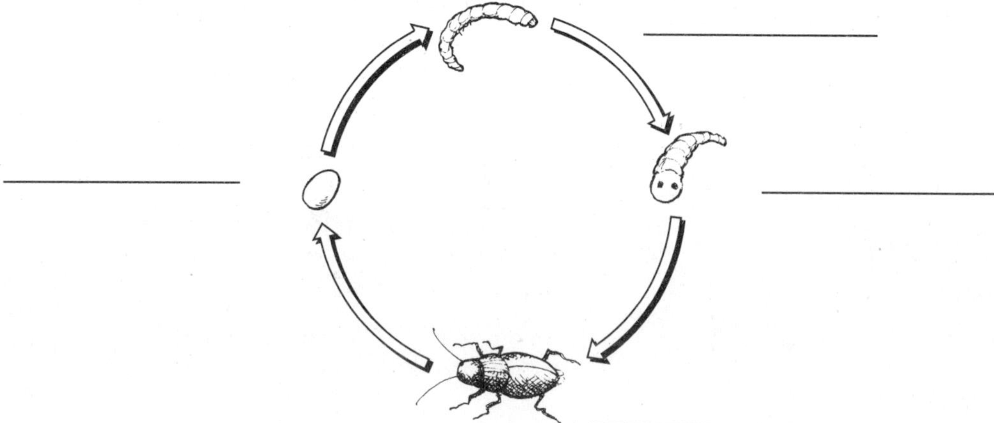

2. Each drawing below represents a stage in the life cycle of a cricket. Label each drawing using the numbers 1, 2, and 3 to show the correct order of the stages.

Process Skills
Communicating, Making Comparisons

On another sheet of paper, write in your own words what happens during the process of incomplete metamorphosis. Compare this with what happens during the process of complete metamorphosis.

____

____

____

Answers on
Assessment Guide p. 147

Unit A • *Life Cycles*

Name _______________________________ Date _______________________

1. Look at the pictures of the baby animals below. Draw a
circle around each baby animal that does not need to be
taken care of by an adult.

2. You have found a very small kitten. Its eyes are open,
but it is not yet able to feed itself. How would you take
care of this kitten?

____

____

____

____

Process Skills
Inferring, Communicating

What kind of care do you think lion parents give to
their cubs? Write your answer on another sheet of paper.

Answers on
Assessment Guide p. 147

Name _________________________________ Date _________________

1. Use the words in the box to correctly label the parts of the seed.

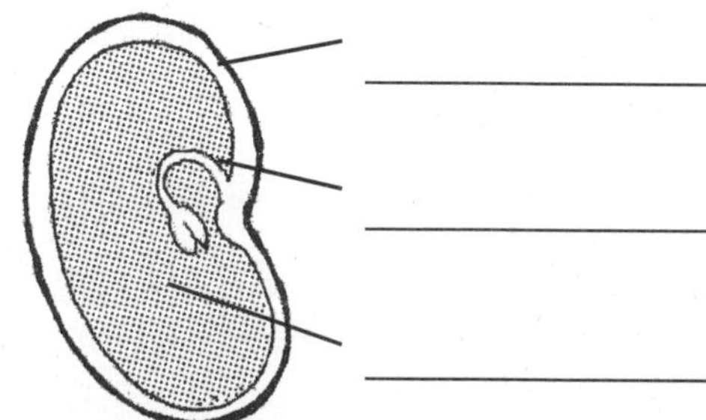

> embryo
>
> seed coat
>
> stored food

2. Use the clues below to unscramble the letters of each word.

   a. The part of a seed that will develop into a plant

     R   M   O   B   E   Y

     ____

   b. The outside layer of a seed

     E   S   E   D   A   C   T   O

     _____________   _____________

   c. The part of a seed that provides nourishment for the developing plant

     O   S   D   E   T   R   O   F   O   D

     _____________   _____________

Process Skills
Classifying

On another sheet of paper, make a chart with three columns. Label the first column *Wind,* the second column *Animals,* and the third column *Water.* Classify the seeds from the plants listed below according to which method the seeds are most likely to be carried away from the parent plant.

dandelion	lotus	acorn
tumbleweed	sticktight	coconut

Answers on
Assessment Guide p. 148

Name _________________________________ Date _______________________

1. Use the words from the box to label the
parts of the flower shown.

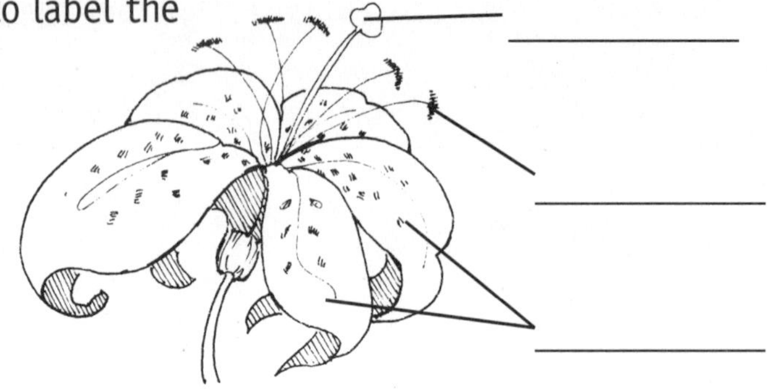

> petals
>
> pistil
>
> stamen

____

____

____

2. Use the words in the box and the clues below to solve the puzzle.

petals	pistil	pollen	stamen

Down

1. Parts of a flower that attract insects

2. Flower part where seeds form

Across

2. Powdery material on a stamen

3. Part of a flower that contains pollen

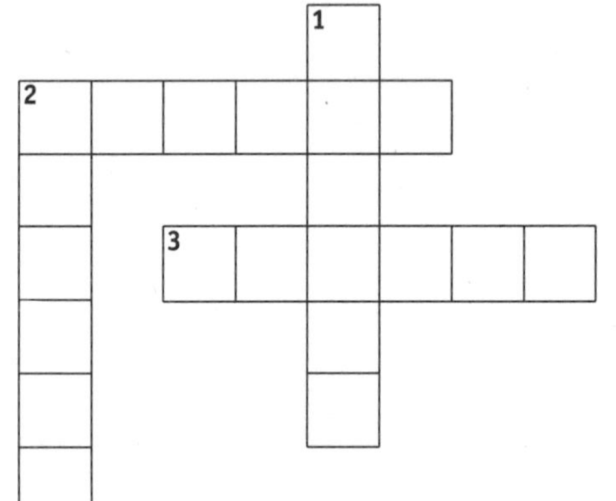

Process Skills
Inferring

Look at the picture of a flower from the coral honeysuckle
vine. Which animal—a bat, a bumblebee, or a hummingbird—
do you think would most likely pollinate this flower? Write
your choice and a reason for your choice on another sheet of
paper.

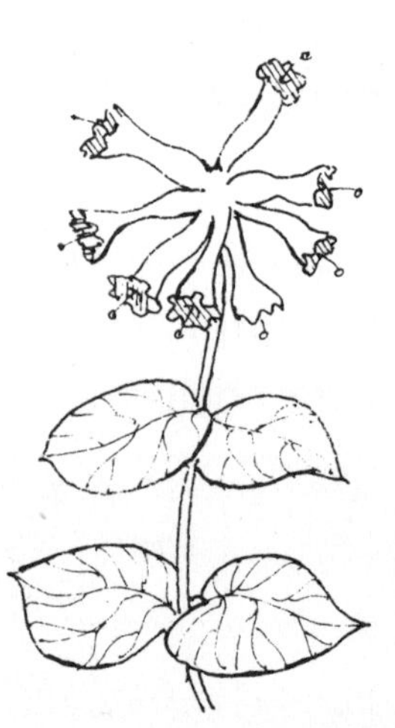

Answers on
Assessment Guide p. 148

Name _________________________________ Date _________________

1. Circle the word or words that best complete each sentence.

   a. (Conifers, Cones, Scales) are plant parts that produce seeds.

   b. Cones are found on trees called (shrubs, vines, conifers).

   c. A cone is made of woody parts called (seeds, stamens, scales).

   d. (Pollen, A seed, A flower) can be found on the scale of a cone.

   e. The cone helps to (nourish, protect, scatter) a conifer's seeds.

2. Use the words in the box to complete the diagram that compares and contrasts flowering plants and conifers.

cones	petals	pollen
scales	seeds	flowers

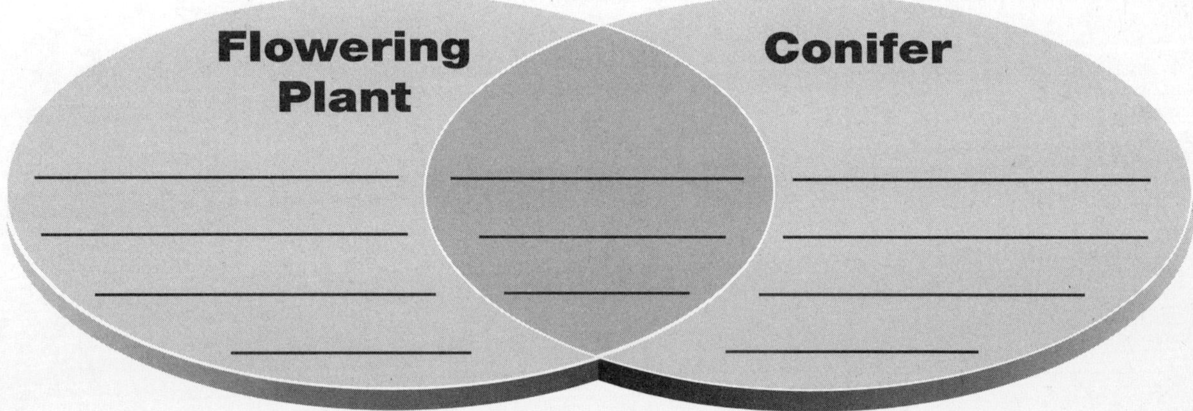

Process Skills
Making Comparisons

Which part of a conifer is most like a stamen in a flower?
Which part of a conifer is most like a pistil in a flower?
Write your answers and the reason for each answer on another sheet of paper.

Answers on
Assessment Guide p. 149

Name _________________________ Date _________________________

1. Answer the following questions on the lines provided.

    a. What does a seedling need to grow besides warmth and moisture?

    ____

    b. How will a seedling grow if it receives light from only one side?

    ____

    c. How will a seedling grow if it receives no light?

    ____

    ____

2. Look at the drawings of the two trees.
Circle the younger tree.

List two things that you observed about the two
trees that helped you choose the younger tree.

____

____

____

____

Process Skills
Inferring, Communicating

Suppose your friend brings you a plant. The stem is
leaning. The leaves are wilted. The soil is dry. Your friend
tells you the plant has been kept in a dark, drafty corner
of a room. What could be done to make the plant
healthy? Write your answer on another sheet of paper.

Answers on
Assessment Guide p. 149

Sun, Moon, and Earth

Name _________________________________ Date _________________

1. Match the term on the left with its definition on the right.

a. telescope — a bowl-shaped pit made when a meteorite collides with an object in space

b. crater — a device with lenses or mirrors that makes faraway objects look larger

c. plain — a chunk of rock or metal from space that lands on a planet or a moon

d. meteorite — a flat area on the Moon's surface formed by melted material that cooled and hardened

2. Use the words and phrases in the box to complete the diagram.

atmosphere	craters	lifeless
gray rocky ball	life	mountains
water	smaller	larger

Earth — **Moon**

_______________ _______________ _______________
_______________ _______________ _______________
_______________   _______________
_______________   _______________

Process Skills
Inferring, Communicating

On another sheet of paper, draw a picture of a big crater and a small crater. Then explain how such features might have formed on the Moon. What might explain the craters' different sizes?

Answers on
Assessment Guide p. 151

Name _________________________ Date _________________

1. Circle the word that best completes each sentence.

  a. (Gravity, Mass) is a pull that every object has on every other object.

  b. The amount of material that makes up an object is its (weight, mass).

  c. The (Sun, Moon) has less mass and therefore less gravitational pull than Earth.

  d. An (astronaut, astronomer) is a person who travels in space or trains for space travel.

2. Place the activities listed in the box in the correct column of the chart below.

| hit a home run | fly a kite | move a pile of bricks |
| swim in a lake | catch a butterfly | observe the stars |

Easier to Do on Earth	Easier to Do on the Moon

Process Skills
Inferring, Communicating

Why does an astronaut need to wear a spacesuit on the Moon? Write your answer on a separate sheet of paper.

Answers on
Assessment Guide p. 151

Name _______________________________ Date _______________

1. Write a definition for each term on the lines below.

　a. sunspot _______________________________

　b. solar flare _______________________________

　c. prominence _______________________________

2. Use the words in the box and the clues below to help you solve the puzzle.

magnetic	northern	storm
star	sunspots	

Down

1. During a solar _______, invisible particles are given off by the Sun.

2. A _______ is a ball of hot gases.

3. Solar storms cause the shimmering colorful display called the _______ lights.

Across

2. Dark patches on the Sun are _______.

4. Solar storms are caused by _______ forces in the Sun.

Process Skills
Making Comparisons

How do Earth and the Sun differ? Write your answer on a separate sheet of paper.

Answers on
Assessment Guide p. 152

Name _______________________________ Date _______________________

1. Look at each sundial and the shadow of the stick in its
center. Draw the Sun above each sundial to show where
the Sun would have to be to cast the shadow.

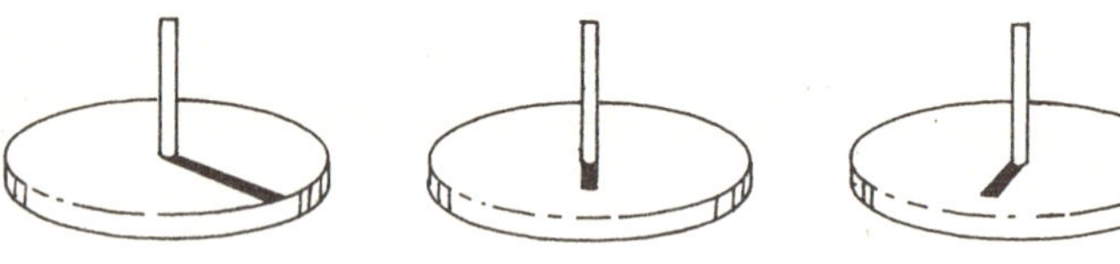

2. Look at each group of words. Put an X on the one word in
each group that does not belong. Use the remaining
words to write a correct sentence.

a. Earth   rotates   day   star

____

____

b. meteorites   constellations   east   west

____

____

c. Little Dipper   Moon   Polaris   north

____

____

Process Skills
Inferring, Communicating

Suppose you are an astronaut in space looking at Earth and
watching the United States. How would the United States
move over the course of 24 hours?

Answers on
Assessment Guide p. 152

Name _________________________________ Date _____________

1. Look at the two scenes below of a lake in the United States. In each scene, draw the Sun to show how it appears to move across the sky during each time of year shown.

2. Use the sentences in the box below to complete the diagram.

Sun is highest in the sky.	Days are short.
Temperatures are coolest.	Sun is lowest in the sky.
Days are long.	Temperatures are warmest.
Earth moves around the Sun.	Earth spins on its axis.

Summer   **Winter**

___________   ___________

___________   ___________

___________   ___________

___________   ___________

Process Skills

Inferring

How could you use the constellations to tell what season it is? Write your answer on a separate sheet of paper.

Answers on
Assessment Guide p. 153

Name _______________________________ Date _______________________

1. Below are three drawings of the Moon. In the first drawing,
shade the portion of the Moon that is dark so it represents a
new Moon. Make the second drawing show a full Moon. Shade
the third drawing so it represents a quarter Moon. Label each
of the drawings.

○   ○   ○

_________   _________   _________

2. Use the words in the box below to complete the sentences.

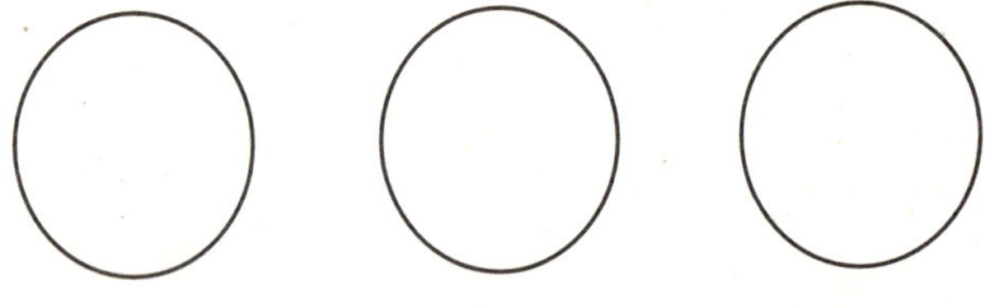

a. The Moon rotates on its __________ .

b. Unlike the Sun, the Moon produces no __________ of its own.

c. The Moon goes through __________ every month.

d. The __________ side of the Moon faces away from Earth.

e. The Moon's gravity makes the oceans rise and fall in daily __________ .

f. The Moon revolves around __________ .

Process Skills
Making and Using Models, Inferring

On a separate sheet of paper, draw a model to show the
positions of the Moon, the Sun, and Earth during a new
Moon. Explain why you can hardly see the Moon at
all during the new Moon phase.

Answers on
Assessment Guide p. 153

Name _________________________________ Date _________________

1. Label the diagram to show fall, spring, summer, and winter for the Northern Hemisphere.

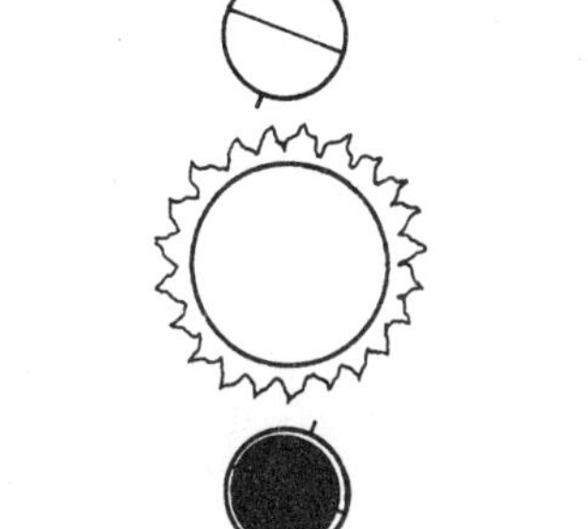

2. Use the words in the box to answer each riddle.

axis	equator	North Pole	Midnight Sun

a. I am an imaginary line that circles Earth. Sunlight always hits directly here, making it warm all the time.

I am the _________________.

b. Earth's axis runs through me. I always point toward Polaris. When sunlight hits me at all, it always hits at

an angle making it cold all the time. I am the _____________.

c. I am an imaginary line running through the center of Earth. I am the _________________.

d. I can be seen in northern Alaska in the middle of the summer, when there are 24 hours of daylight each

day. I am the _________________.

Process Skills
Inferring

Suppose you will be spending December and January with some friends in Australia. What kinds of clothes should you take? Why? Write your answer on a separate sheet of paper.

Answers on
Assessment Guide p. 154

Name _________________________________ Date _________________

1. In diagram A, draw the Moon in the position it must be in for a solar eclipse to occur. In diagram B, draw the Moon in the position it must be in for a lunar eclipse to occur.

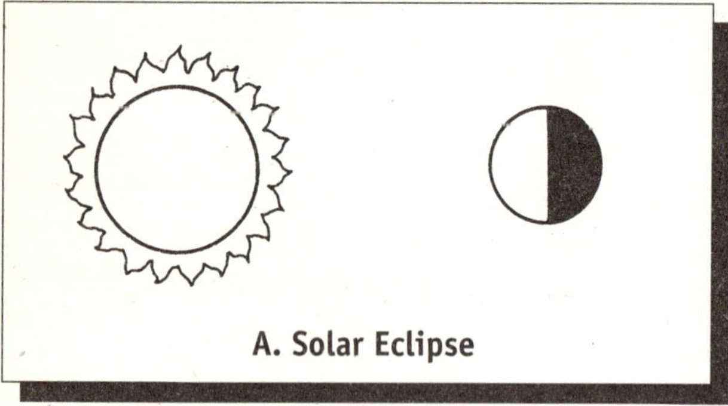

A. Solar Eclipse

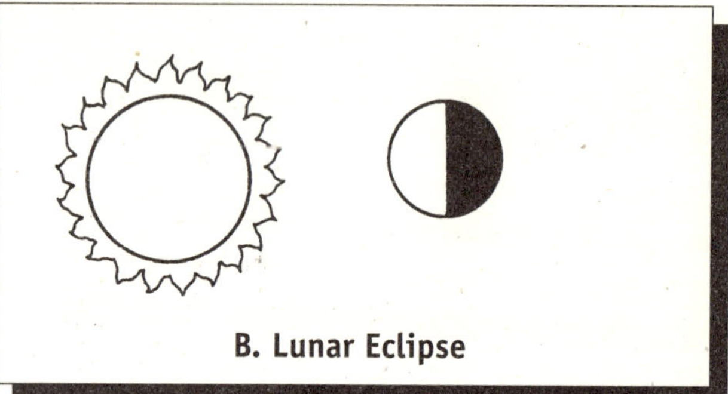

B. Lunar Eclipse

2. Write *L* on the line in front of each phrase or statement that represents a fact about a lunar eclipse. Write *S* on the line in front of each phrase or statement that represents a fact about a solar eclipse.

a. _________ The Moon seems to darken.

b. _________ The Sun is blocked from view.

c. _________ The Sun seems to darken.

d. _________ It occurs when the Moon's shadow falls on Earth.

e. _________ It occurs when Earth's shadow falls on the Moon.

Process Skills
Communicating

On a separate sheet of paper, write a definition for a solar eclipse. Describe what you would observe during a total solar eclipse.

Answers on
Assessment Guide p. 154

FORMS OF ENERGY

Name ________________________________ Date ________________________

1. Circle the letter of the word or phrase that best completes
each sentence.

A. The energy that moving matter has is called ____.

   a. stored energy   **c.** energy of motion

   b. light energy   **d.** energy of matter

B. Chemical energy is stored in ____.

   a. light   **b.** sound   **c.** fuels   **d.** wind

2. Draw a line from the example of energy shown to at least
one kind of energy it represents.

    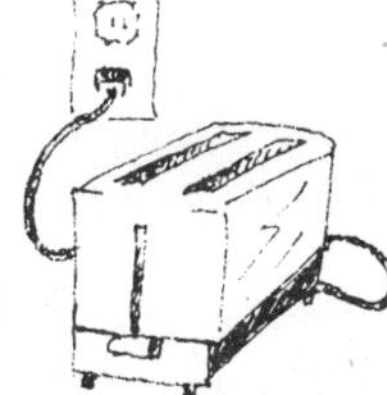

sound   electrical   mechanical   heat   light

Process Skills
Predicting, Making a Hypothesis

Maria is playing with her toy airplane. One end of a rubber
band is attached to the propeller. The other end is attached
to the body of the airplane. Maria turns the propeller to wind
the rubber band. She raises the airplane high above her
head. She lets go of the airplane. Predict what will happen
and hypothesize why this happens. What energy change
takes place when Maria lets go of the airplane? Write your
answers on a separate sheet of paper.

Answers on
Assessment Guide p. 156

Name _________________________________ Date _________________________

1. Circle the word or phrase that best completes each sentence.

   a. When an eraser is rubbed back and forth many times,
   some of the energy of motion is changed to
   _____________ energy.

   light   heat   stored

   b. When a match is burning, the energy _____________.

   is lost   changes form   increases

2. Use the words and clues to help you complete the puzzle.
Then use the circled letters to answer the riddle below.

electrical	light	mechanical	solar

   a. When a bulb burns brightly,
   electrical energy has been
   changed to _____________ energy.   _ _ _ Ⓞ _

   b. When a wind-up toy moves,
   stored energy changes to
   _____________ energy.   _ Ⓞ _ _ _ _ _ _ _ _

   c. Energy from the Sun is called
   _____________ energy.   _ _ _ Ⓞ _

   d. A computer uses _____________
   energy.   _ _ _ _ Ⓞ _ _ _ _

What is often given off when energy changes from one form
to another form? _____________

Process Skills
Inferring, Communicating

Explain how energy changes in a campfire.
Write your answer on a separate sheet of paper.

Answers on
Assessment Guide p. 156

Name _________________________________ Date _________________________

1. Draw a line on straw A to show where the water level would be when the bottle thermometer is placed in ice water. Draw a line on straw B to show where the water level would be when the bottle thermometer is placed in hot water. Then explain why you drew your lines where you did.

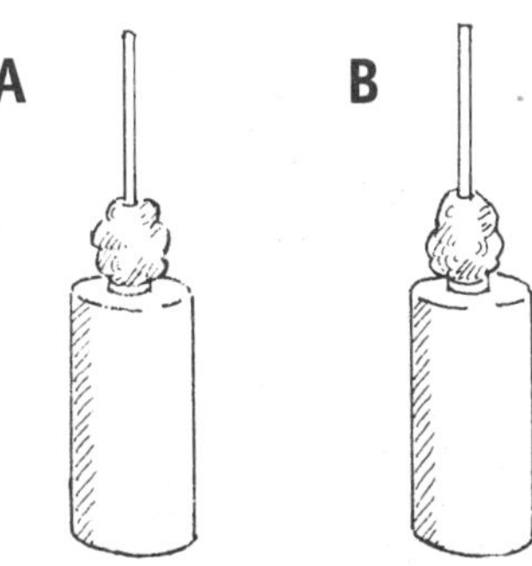

____

____

____

2. Draw a line from each picture to the term or phrase that best describes the picture.

helium balloon   sick in bed   particles are close together   rubbing cold hands together   particles take the shape of the container but can't move out of the container.

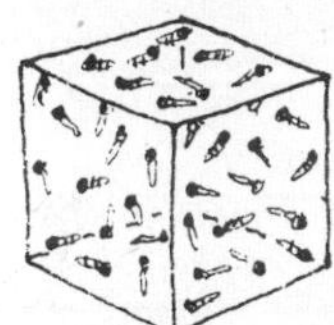

measuring temperature   gas   liquid   solid   friction

Process Skills
Inferring

It is a cold day in winter when you buy some gas-filled balloons for a party at your home. You walk home carrying the floating balloons. As you walk you notice that the balloons are barely floating and are shrinking in size. But after 15 minutes in your warm home, the balloons look as they did when you first bought them. What caused these changes in the balloons? Explain. Write your answer on a separate sheet of paper.

Answers on
Assessment Guide p. 157

Unit C • *Forms of Energy*   **29**

Name _________________________ Date _________________________

1. Circle the drawings that show good conductors of heat.

metal kettle   wood   down jacket   aluminum foil

2. Use the phrases in the box to help you complete the diagram below.

transfer of heat	needs particles of matter
does not need matter	involves invisible waves
warm particles move upward	moves through a vacuum

Convection   **Radiation**

Process Skills
Comparing and Contrasting

Compare and contrast how heat travels through solids, liquids, and gases. Write your answer on a separate sheet of paper.

Answers on
Assessment Guide p. 157

Name ____________________ Date ____________________

A   B

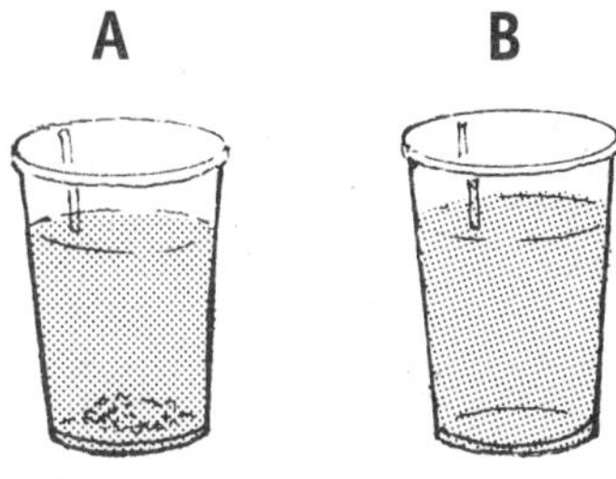

1. Look at the two glasses of tea. One is cold tea and one is warm tea. Three teaspoons of sugar were added to each glass, and the the tea was stirred. Which glass contains the cold tea? How do you know?

____

____

2. Read the story below. Then answer the question.

It is a very warm, sunny, spring day. The lake water is still cold from the long winter. A young man accidentally slips and falls into the lake. He quickly gets out and is not hurt. However, his clothes are soaking wet.

Would the man warm up quickly if he sat in the Sun? Explain.

____

____

____

____

Process Skills
Inferring

Look at the summer scene. Tell where the processes of melting, evaporating, condensing, and freezing are taking place or have taken place. Write your answer on a separate sheet of paper.

Answers on
Assessment Guide p. 158

Unit C • *Forms of Energy*   **31**

Name _________________________________ Date _________________

1. Use the words in the box to complete the sentences.

fossil fuels	geothermal energy	nuclear energy

a. _____________________________ comes from deep within Earth and is used in some areas to heat homes.

b. _________________ include coal, oil, and natural gas.

c. A source of energy that leaves behind radioactive wastes is

_____________________.

2. Use the phrases in the box to complete the diagram.

cause air pollution	cause no air pollution	heat houses
limited supplies	vast or endless supplies	used widely now
future energy sources	produce electricity	

Fossil Fuels

Alternative Energy Sources

_____________ _____________ _____________

_____________ _____________ _____________

_____________ _____________

Process Skills
Inferring, Communicating

Where does the energy used to heat your school come from? How does the heat energy get to you? Write your answers on a separate sheet of paper.

Answers on
Assessment Guide p. 158

Name _________________________________ Date _________________________

1. Sequence these steps to explain how coal forms.

_____ Extreme heat and pressure changed the bituminous coal to anthracite.

_____ Over millions of years, the mass of these layers changed the dead plants into peat then lignite.

_____ Millions of years ago swamp plants died and fell to the swamp floor.

_____ Over more time, the lignite changed to bituminous coal.

_____ Layers of sand and other debris covered the plant matter.

2. Study the drawings. Order the materials below from the one that best keeps the heat in to the one that lets most of the heat escape. Then answer the question.

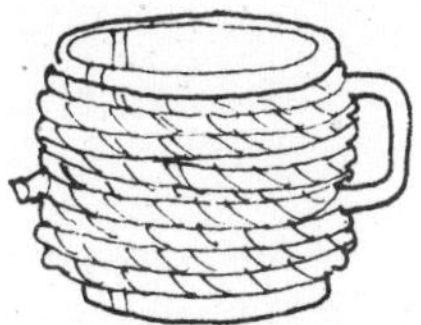

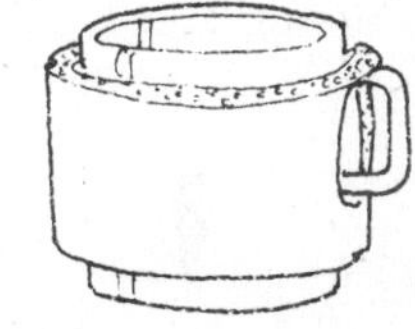

_____ Thick wool yarn   _____ Thin cotton cloth   _____ Plastic foam

A thermos bottle helps keep hot things hot and cold things cold. Which of the insulating materials above would you expect to find in a thermos bottle? _________________________

Process Skills
Communicating

How can you help save energy?
Write your answer on a separate sheet of paper.

Answers on
Assessment Guide p. 159

EARTH'S WATER

Name _________________________ Date _________________

1. a. Shade the part of the graph that shows how much of Earth's water is salt water.

b. What does the unshaded part of the graph represent?

____

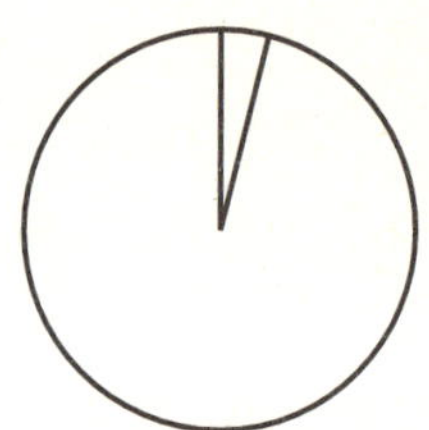

c. Draw a pie graph to show how much of Earth's surface is water and how much is land. Shade in the part of your pie graph that shows how much of Earth's surface is water.

2. Use the words in the box to complete the puzzle.

glaciers	living things	resources	salt	survive	water

Across

2. All living things need water to ___.

4. Earth is sometimes called the ___ planet.

5. I make food tasty, but I make water unfit to drink. I am ___.

Down

1. Air, soil, and water are natural ___.

3. Most of Earth's fresh water is frozen in icecaps, ___, and icebergs.

6. All ___ contain water.

Process Skills
Communicating

Earth is the only planet known to have liquid water, and all living things need water. Is it likely that other planets, such as Mars, have life? Explain your answer on a separate sheet of paper.

Answers on
Assessment Guide p. 161

Name _________________________________ Date _______________________

1. In the activity, "Water Ups and Downs," you made a model of the water cycle. Picture A looks like the model you made. Picture B shows a lake near the base of some mountains.

a. Draw an arrow from water droplets on the foil to the item in Picture B that this water best represents.

b. On Picture A and on Picture B, draw an X on the place where evaporation occurs.

c. On Picture A and on Picture B, draw a star on the place where condensation occurs.

2. Use the words in the box to complete the sentences.

condenses	cycle	evaporates	gas

a. Water moves in nature through a _________________.

b. When you add heat to liquid water, the water _________________ and becomes a gas.

c. Water vapor is a _________________.

d. Water vapor changes to a liquid when it _________________.

Process Skills
Hypothesizing

From which pond would water evaporate more quickly? Explain your answer on a separate sheet of paper.

Answers on
Assessment Guide p. 161

Name _________________________________ Date _________________________

1. Use the words in the box to complete each sentence.

| surface water   ground water   reservoir   aquifer |

a. Rivers and lakes supply people with _________________.

b. An underground layer of rock where ground water collects is called an

_________________.

c. Water that soaks into the ground and fills the spaces between soil

and rocks is called _________________.

d. A place where water is collected and stored is called a _________________.

2. The drawings show a cross section of the ground at three places.
At which place, A, B, or C, would you drill a water well? Explain.

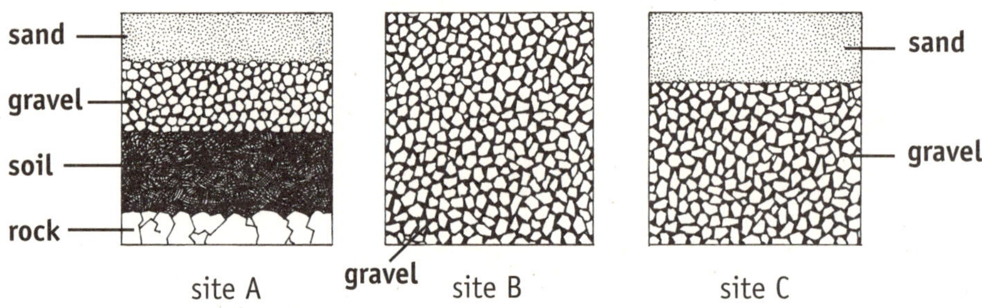

____

____

Process Skills
Predicting

Two towns get all their fresh water from the same reservoir.
Together, the towns use water equal to the rate at which
water collects in the reservoir. What will happen if a third
town begins to use the reservoir as a water source? Write
your prediction on a separate sheet of paper.

Answers on
Assessment Guide p. 161

Name _______________________________________ Date _______________________

1. Circle the letter of the word or phrase to complete each sentence.

   A. Water flows through pipes in your home because of ____.

      a. temperature   **c.** ground water

      b. water pressure   **d.** expansion

   B. Water flows from a water tower because of ____.

      a. gravity   **c.** ground water

      b. temperature   **d.** expansion

   C. The reason water mains are buried in the ground is ____.

      a. so the water coming to your home is cold

      b. to prevent water from freezing during the winter

      c. to increase the water pressure

      d. to avoid flooding

2. The five statements below tell how water comes to many homes. These statements, however, are not in the right order. Put the statements in the correct order.

   ____ Water from a water source goes to a treatment plant.

   ____ Submains branch to every street.

   ____ A pumping station pumps water under pressure to water mains.

   ____ Water is pumped out of a water source.

   ____ Pipes from submains go to every building, including your home.

Process Skills
Inferring

What is the relationship between how much water is in a water tower and how fast the water will flow through the pipe leading from the tower? Write your answer on a separate sheet of paper.

Answers on
Assessment Guide p. 162

Name _________________________________ Date _______________________

1. Circle the word that best completes each sentence.

a. Water that does not make a lot of suds when detergent is added to it is (hard, soft) water.

b. Some people "treat" (hard, soft) water by running it through a water softener.

c. If you like to take bubble baths with lots of bubbles, you should use (hard, soft) water.

d. Most people prefer the taste of water that has (some, no) dissolved minerals in it.

2. The harder the water, the more minerals it has dissolved in it. Read the descriptions of the water samples. Then answer the questions.

SAMPLE A: Water collected from a mineral spring at Yellowstone National Park

SAMPLE B: Rainwater

SAMPLE C: Distilled Water

a. Which sample would probably contain the most dissolved minerals? _______________

b. Which sample(s) would probably contain the least dissolved minerals? _______________

c. Which sample(s) would most likely be labeled "soft water"? _______________

d. Which sample might be labeled "hard water"?

____

Process Skills
Making and Using a Model, Hypothesizing

How could you demonstrate that hard water and soft water are different? Write your answer on a separate sheet of paper.

Answers on
Assessment Guide p. 162

Name _________________________________ Date _________________

1. Use the words in the box to complete the sentences.

boiling	filtering	chemicals
germs	soil	

Water from Earth's surface can contain leaves, insects, and _________________ which makes the water look muddy. These items can be removed by

_________________. In addition, water can contain tiny living things,

called _________________, that can make people sick. They can be removed

by _________________. They may also be killed by treating water with

_________________.

2. The statements below tell how a water treatment plant cleans water. These statements, however, are not in the right order. Put the statements in the correct order.

_____ Chlorine is added to disinfect the water.

_____ The water is passed through a sand and gravel filter.

_____ Water from a source is pumped through a screen.

_____ Water goes to a settling tank where alum is added and forms floc.

Process Skills
Inferring

Mary and Sally are camping in the wilderness. They both eat and drink the same things. Mary, however, drinks some water directly from a nearby lake, while Sally boils the water to make tea. Why might Mary become ill? Write your answer on a separate sheet of paper.

Answers on
Assessment Guide p. 163

Name _______________________   Date _______________________

1. Look at the picture. Put an X on the things that are
causing or could cause water pollution.

2. Use the words in the box to complete the sentences.

acid rain	polluted	germs	chemicals

A body of water that is ___________ contains unwanted or harmful materials.
Smoke can combine with moisture in the air to form ___________ which can fall in
bodies of water. The Safe Drinking Water Act passed by Congress sets limits for the
amount of _______ and ___________ allowed in drinking water.

Process Skills
Identifying Variables, Making a Hypothesis

Your cousin asks you why the fish are dying in a river near his
house. What might you ask him before you form a hypothesis?
Write the questions on a separate sheet of paper.

Answers on
Assessment Guide p. 163

Name _______________________________________ Date _______________________

1. Circle the word that best completes each sentence.

    a. (Currents, Tides) can form as the wind blows over the surface of water.

    b. Steady winds that blow from one region of the world to another region cause (deep-ocean currents, surface currents).

    c. The moon pulls on Earth's surface, causing (tides, surface currents).

    d. When warm water rises and cold water sinks, (waves, deep-ocean currents) are formed.

2. Study the drawing. Then answer the questions below.

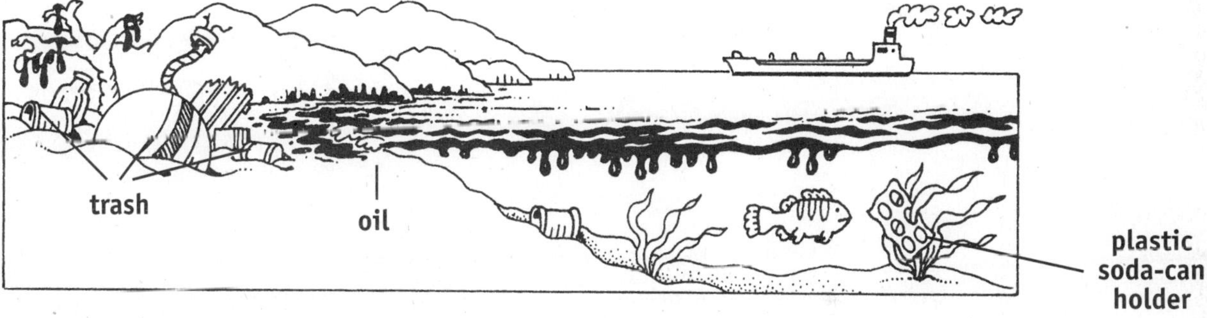

    a. How did the oil get so far up on the beach and on the rocks?

    ____

    b. Look at the plants growing on the bottom of the ocean floor. How did the plastic soda-can holder get from the beach to the plants?

    ____

    ____

Process Skills
Observing

Suppose you could visit Chesapeake Bay. How could you tell that efforts at cleaning up Chesapeake Bay are working? Write your answer on a separate sheet of paper.

Answers on
Assessment Guide p. 164

Name _______________________________ Date _______________

1. Put an X over the drawings that show water being wasted.

brushing teeth

washing a
full load

taking a
5-minute shower

washing a car

2. Use the activities listed in the box to complete the chart.

> running the faucet to get cold water
> taking a long shower
> taking a bath when the tub is only
>   partly filled
>
> fixing a leaky faucet
> watering the lawn at noon
> doing full loads of laundry

Conserving Water	Wasting Water

Process Skills
Collecting and Recording Data

If a friend asked you to find a way to reduce her family's
water bill, what is the first thing you would do? Write your
answer on a separate sheet of paper.

Answers on
Assessment Guide p. 164

ROLES OF LIVING THINGS

Name ___________________________________ Date ___________________

1. Match the animal on the left with its environment on the right.

    a. whale   soil

    b. bass   rain forest

    c. earthworm   desert

    d. cactus   ocean

    e. squirrel monkey   lake

2. Use the words in the box to complete the diagram that compares and contrasts what an orchid and a cactus need to live. An orchid is a flowering plant that grows on the branches of different trees in a rain forest.

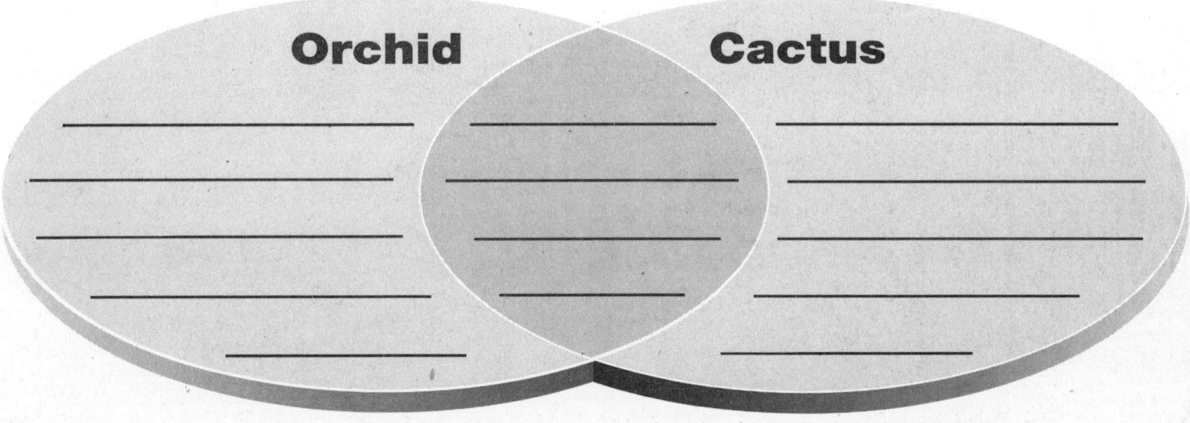

Process Skills
Making Comparisons, Interpreting Data

Compare and contrast the things young plants and earthworms need to live. Write your answer on a separate sheet of paper.

Answers on
Assessment Guide p. 166

Name _______________________________ Date _______________________

1. Use a word from the box to fill in each blank.

herbivores	plants	omnivores
carnivores	animals	

The foods most people eat come from _______________ and _______________.
Animals that eat only plants are called _______________. Animals that eat only
other animals are called _______________. Animals that eat both plants and animals
are called _______________.

2. Use the words in the box and the clues below to complete the puzzle.

food	tiny	living	mold	moist

Down

1. Mold grows on bread and fruit
and uses these as _______.

2. Mold often grows in places
that are dark and _______.

3. Molds are _______ things.

Across

2. _______ is a fuzzy-looking
organism that can be found
growing on food.

4. Molds are very _______.

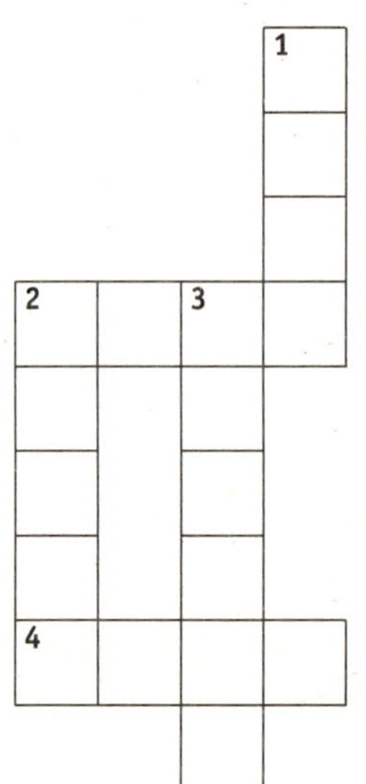

Process Skills
Observing

How could you find out whether an animal was a herbivore, a
carnivore, or an omnivore? Write your answer on a separate
sheet of paper.

Answers on
Assessment Guide p. 166

Name _______________________ Date _______________________

1. Use the names of the living things in the box to fill in the rectangles that make a food chain. Then answer the questions below.

| mouse | mountain lion | fox | grass |

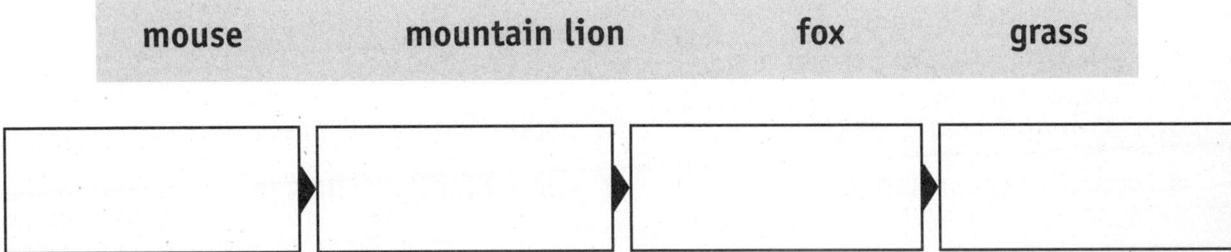

    a. Which living things in the food chain are prey? _______________

    b. Which living things are predators? _______________

2. Look at the drawing below. Draw an arrow from each living thing to the living thing that eats it. Then fill in the blank in the sentence below.

Many food chains can be linked to form a _______________.

Process Skills
Making a Model

How might making a model have helped prevent the cane toad problem in Australia? Write your answer on a separate sheet of paper.

Answers on
Assessment Guide p. 167

Unit E • *Roles of Living Things*

Name _________________________ Date _________________________

1. Draw a line from the adaptation on the left to the phrase that describes how it helps the animal.

a. chameleon's eyes   trap tiny plants, shrimp, and snails

b. hummingbird's long   watch for predator and prey at
beak and tongue   same time

c. flamingos' large beaks   paralyze and kill prey

d. snake's poison fangs   sip nectar from flower

2. Unscramble the words to help you complete the sentences.

a. I am a hawk. Even though I fly high in the sky, I use my sharp ____ to spot a mouse way below.

Y S E T E I H G _________________

b. I am a sea otter. I get some of my food because I am able to use a rock as a ____.

O L O T _________________

c. I am a lioness. I can catch a gazelle by behaving in a certain way. I ____ , or secretly follow and sneak up on, my prey.

T L K S A _________________

d. Animals in nature must work hard to get food. Their task is made easier by their ____.

P T T O N A D S A I A _________________

Process Skills
Hypothesizing

Hypothesize why owls, bats, and other night hunters have highly developed senses of hearing. Write your hypothesis on a separate sheet of paper.

Answers on
Assessment Guide p. 167

Name _________________________________ Date _________________

1. Circle the word that best completes each sentence.

    a. The adaptations of a rose that protect it are found on the _____ .

        leaves   stems   flowers

    b. The adaptations of a holly plant that protect it are found on the _____ .

        leaves   stems   flowers

    c. When the pill bug rolls into a ball, its _____ outer shell protects its tender underside.

        soft   smelly   hard

    d. A brown moth lands on the bark of a tree. The moth blends into the bark and seems to disappear because of the moth's _____ .

        size   shape   color

2. Match the picture with the word or phrase that describes the adaptation.

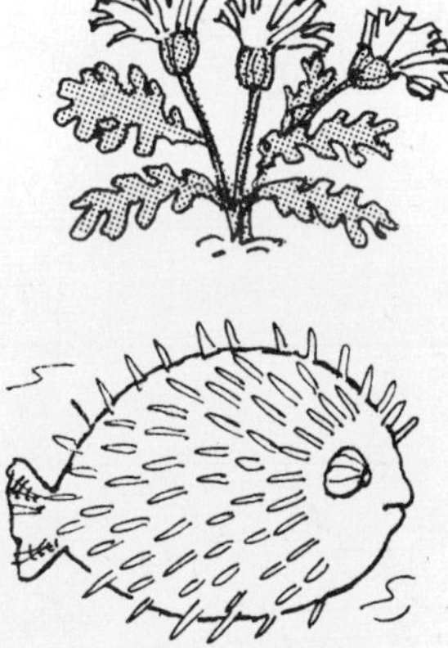

camouflage

copy cat

bitter taste

spines

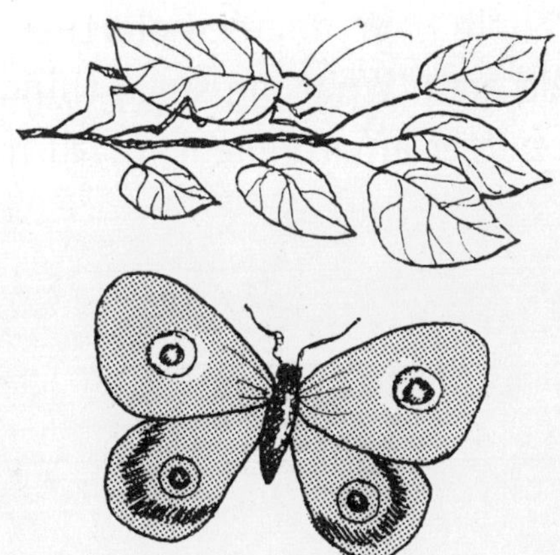

Process Skills
Communicating

How did the insect model you made help you understand adaptations of living things? Write your answer on a separate sheet of paper.

Answers on
Assessment Guide p. 168

Unit E • *Roles of Living Things*

Name _______________________________ Date _______________________

1. Look at the picture. Then answer the questions below.

a. What changes are taking place that improve the environment?

____

b. What changes are taking place that harm the environment?

____

2. There is an area in your neighborhood that has become polluted.
People have dumped old tires, aluminum cans, and other trash in
the area. What are some things you can do to help make the area
a better environment for all the living things in the neighborhood?

____

____

____

Process Skills
Predicting

You are walking along a stream and you see some new
arrivals to the area—beavers. Predict what will happen to
the plant life in the area. Write your answer on a separate
sheet of paper.

Answers on
Assessment Guide p. 168

Name _______________________________ Date _______________________

1. Circle the sentence about the desert that is **NOT** true.

 a. Stilt beetles keep cool by tiptoeing across the hot sand.

 b. Many desert animals sweat, which keeps them cool.

 c. A kangaroo rat may go its entire life without drinking water.

 d. The white wax on desert beetles reflects the sun and keeps in moisture.

2. Animals and plants have many different ways to deal with harsh environments or changes in their environments. Match the animal or plant on the left with its adaptation on the right. Then answer the question below.

_____ goose	**a.** stays in its burrow during the day
_____ kangaroo rat	**b.** loses its leaves
_____ cactus	**c.** hibernates
_____ ground squirrel	**d.** migrates
_____ oak	**e.** grows slender, spiny leaves

What special adaptation do you have to help you deal with hot, summer weather?

____

____

Process Skills
Making a Model

What did making a model of a bird tell you about how a bird protects itself from the cold?

____

____

Answers on
Assessment Guide p. 169

WHAT'S FOR LUNCH?

Name _________________________________ Date _______________

1. Use the words in the box to complete the sentences.

fats	nutrients	proteins	starch	water

Foods contain _________________ that the body uses for energy, growth, and repair. Your body needs carbohydrates, such as _____________, for energy. Your body uses _______________ not only for energy but also to help keep your body warm. For growth and repair, your body especially needs _____________. You also need a lot of _____________ to carry out all of the important body processes.

2. In the box below are foods that are high in one or more kinds of nutrients. List these foods in the correct column in the chart. Some foods may be listed more than once.

bread	broccoli	butter	chicken
fish	honey	oranges	peanut butter

Carbohydrates	Fats	Proteins	Vitamins	Minerals

Process Skills
Inferring

Suppose you are buying a loaf of bread and six chocolate-chip cookies at a bakery. The baker put the cookies in a wax-coated bag and the bread in a brown paper bag. Explain why on a separate sheet of paper.

Answers on
Assessment Guide p. 171

Name _____________________________ Date _____________________

1. Label the food groups for the Food Guide Pyramid below.

___________________   ___________________

___________________   ___________________

___________________   ___________________

___________________   ___________________

2. Look at the types of foods that make up this lunch. In the chart below, tell how many servings from each food group there are.

a. Breads, cereals, rice, and pasta _____________.

b. Vegetables _____________.

c. Fruits _____________.

d. Milk, yogurt, and cheese _____________.

e. Meat, poultry, fish, and eggs _____________.

Process Skills
Making Comparisons, Inferring

Joey is so hungry! He eats a handful of potato chips and a candy bar. Joey is also thirsty. Then he drinks a can of diet soda. How would you rate Joey's choice of foods? What different foods might Joey choose to be more healthful? Write your answers on another sheet of paper.

Answers on
Assessment Guide p. 171

Name _________________________ **Date** _________________________

1. Look at the foods below. Put an X on foods that are high in fat, sugar, salt, and Calories, and low in nutrients.

French fries   **hot dog**   **grapes**   **doughnut**   **yogurt**   **broccoli**

2. Compare the two labels from boxes of cereal. Then answer the questions below.

Which cereal contains more sugar per serving? _______

Which cereal contains more fat per serving? _______

Which cereal contains more sodium per serving? _______

Which cereal contains more Calories per serving?

____

____

Which cereal is healthier? _______

Nutrition Facts

Serving Size		3/4 cup (30 g/1.1 oz)
Servings Per Package		11

Amount Per Serving	Cereal	Cereal with 1/2 cup Vitamins A & D Skim Milk
Calories	120	160
Calories from Fat	15	15

	% Daily Value**	
Total Fat 2.0 g*	3%	3%
Saturated Fat 1.0 g	5%	5%
Cholesterol 0 mg	0%	0%
Sodium 210 mg	9%	11%
Potassium 45 mg	1%	7%
Total Carbohydrate 24 g	8%	10%
Dietary Fiber 1 g	4%	4%
Sugars 9 g		
Other Carbohydrate 14 g		
Protein 2 g		

A

Nutrition Facts

Serving Size: 3/4 cup (30 g)
Servings Per Container: 15 Servings

Amount Per Serving

Calories 120 Calories from Fat 10

	% Daily Value*
Total Fat 1 g	2%
Saturated Fat 0 g	2%
Cholesterol 0 mg	2%
Sodium 115 mg	2%
Total Carbohydrate 25 g	8%
Fiber 1 g	4%
Sugars 3 g	
Protein 2 g	

B

Process Skills
Inferring

Suppose you are shopping for lunch meat in a grocery store. What information on the labels of the packages of lunch meat will you look at to decide which package of lunch meat is healthier? Write your answer on another sheet of paper.

Answers on
Assessment Guide p. 171

Name _________________________________ Date _________________

1. Use the words in the box to correctly complete each sentence.

cough	bacteria	temperatures
	hot	cold

People can get sick by eating food that has germs, or ______________, growing on it. To help keep germs off food, you should wash your hands with ______________ soapy water before and after preparing food. You should never sneeze or ______________ over food. You should keep foods ________ to slow down the growth of bacteria. Cooking foods at high ______________ kill bacteria.

2. Identify foods that are safe to eat by writing *S* on the line before that food. If you think the food is not safe to eat, write *N* on the line in front of it.

________ Potato salad left on the kitchen counter all day

________ An orange that has been sitting in a fruit bowl for two days

________ A hamburger that is pink in the middle

________ A slice of cheese that has fallen on the kitchen floor

________ A piece of leftover, fully cooked chicken kept cold in the refrigerator for one day

Process Skills
Predicting

Raw milk is not processed in any way. Pasteurized milk is treated at high temperatures. Which kind of milk do you think would be safer to drink? Explain. Write your answer and explanation on another sheet of paper.

Answers on
Assessment Guide p. 172

Name _________________________________ Date _____________________

1. Use the words in the box to label the diagram.

esophagus	salivary gland	tooth
tongue	palate	

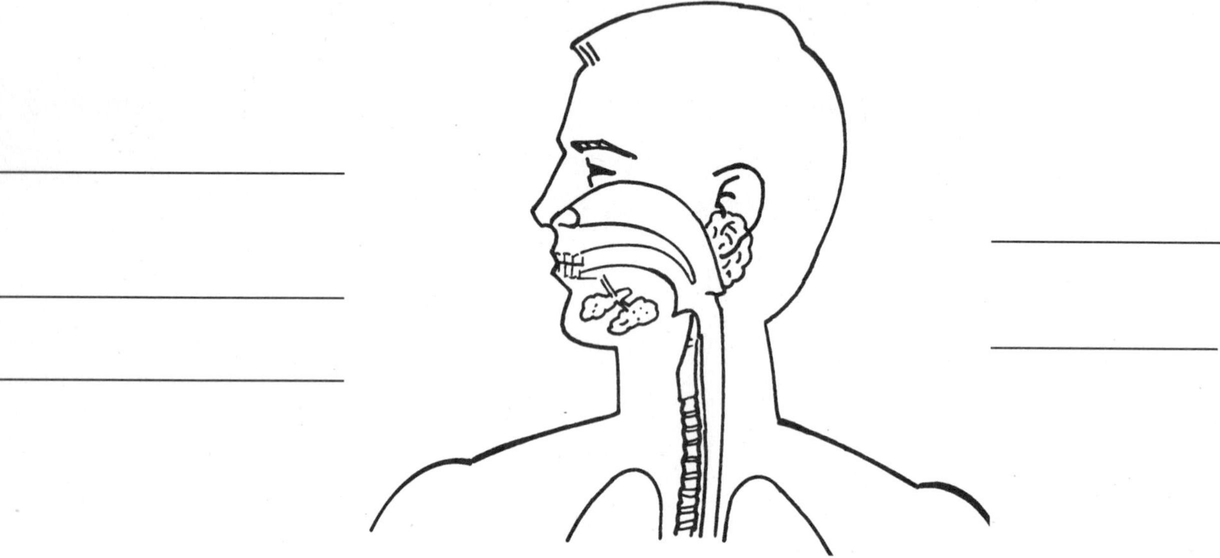

2. Read the steps that describe chewing and swallowing food. The steps are not in the correct order. Number the steps in the correct order.

________ Food enters the stomach.

________ Food moves to the back of the throat.

________ Saliva mixes with food.

________ A small flap of skin covers the opening to the windpipe.

________ A piece of food is bitten off.

________ Food moves down the esophagus.

Process Skills
Inferring

Would you be able to tell the difference between an onion and a piece of chocolate if you did not have any taste buds? Explain. Write your answer on a separate sheet of paper.

Answers on
Assessment Guide p. 172

Investigation Review
How Can You Keep Your Teeth Healthy?

Name _______________________________ Date _______________________________

1. On the diagram, identify one of
each of the following kinds of teeth:
canine, incisor, molar, premolar.

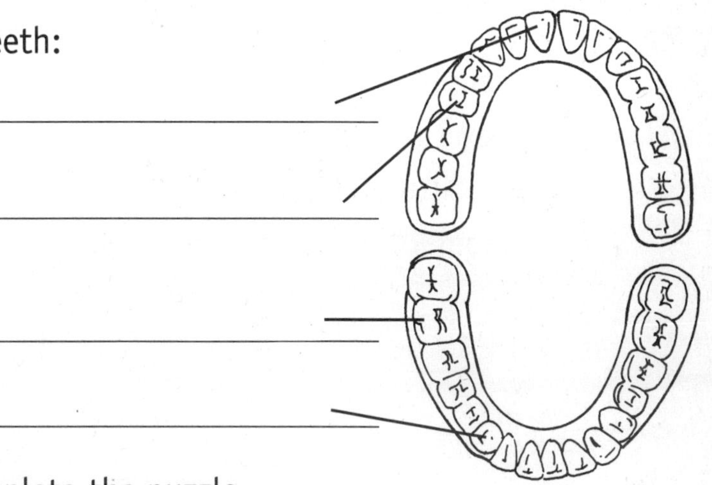

____

____

____

____

2. Use the words in the box to complete the puzzle.

brush	incisors	premolars	canines	floss	teeth

Down

1. Your _______ are designed to cut,
tear, crush, and grind food.

2. Dental _______ removes food between
your teeth and gums.

3. You have two _______ on the top and
two on the bottom.

5. After eating, you should _______ your
teeth with a soft-bristled
toothbrush.

Across

4. Your _______ grind and crush food.

6. Your _______ bite and tear food.

Process Skills
Predicting

How would your diet change if you were missing all of your
premolars and molars? Write your answers on a separate
sheet of paper.

Answers on
Assessment Guide p. 173

Name _______________________ Date _______________

1. Use the words in the box to label the diagram.

esophagus
large intestine
small intestine
stomach

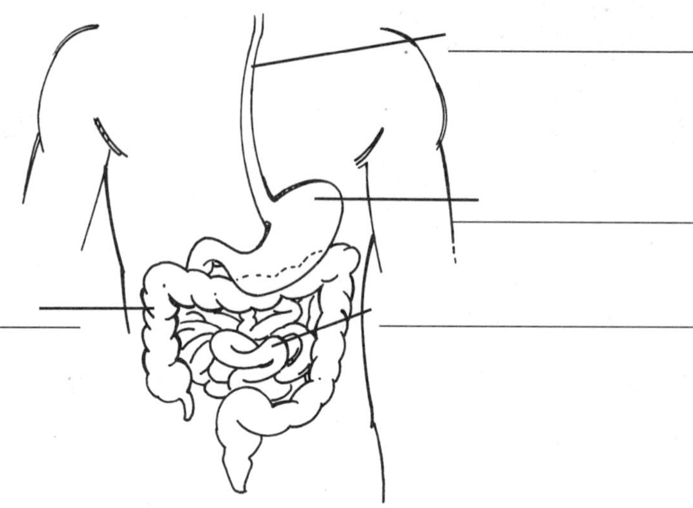

2. Use the words in the box to complete the diagram that compares the different parts of the digestive system.

large intestine   mouth   small intestine   stomach

Where Digestion Occurs

Where Nutrients Are Absorbed

Process Skills
Making and Using a Model

On another sheet of paper, list, in order, the body parts that food passes through from the time it enters the body to when wastes leave the body. Connect the name of each body part with arrows. Begin with the mouth.

Answers on
Assessment Guide p. 173